MADELINE'S CHRISTMAS
by Ludwig Bemelmans

In an old house in Paris that was covered with vines

Lived twelve little girls in two straight lines.

They left the house at half-past nine

In two straight lines, in rain or shine.

The smallest one was MADELINE.

She was not afraid of mice

She loved winter, snow and ice

And to the tiger in the zoo

Madeline just said . . . "POOH, POOH!"

It was the night before Christmas

And all through the house

Not a creature was stirring

Not even the mouse.

For like everyone else in that house which was old

The poor mouse was in bed with a miserable cold.

And only our brave little Madeline

Was up and about and feeling just fine.

Suddenly came a knock which made her pause—

Could it perhaps be Santa Claus?

But no . . .

A rug merchant was at the door.

He had twelve rugs, he had no more.

"Why these," said Madeline, "would be so neat

For our ice-cold in the morning feet."

"It seems to me," said Miss Clavel,

"That you have chosen very well."

Madeline gave him a handful of francs,

"Here they are with all our thanks."

Without the rugs which he had sold

The rug merchant got awfully cold.

"To sell my rugs," he cried, "was silly!

Without them I am very chilly."

He wants to get them back—

But will he?

He made it—back to Madeline's door—

He couldn't take one footstep more.

And little Madeline set about

To find a way to thaw him out.

The merchant, who was tall and thin

(And also a ma-gi-ci-an)

Bravely took his medicine.

The magician, as he took his pill,

Said, "Ask me, Madeline, what you will."

Said she, "I've cooked a dinner nutritious,

Will you please help me with these dishes?"

"If you'll clear up I'll go and see

If I can find a Christmas tree."

His magic ring he gave a glance

And went into a special trance—

The dirty dishes washed themselves

And jumped right back upon the shelves.

And then he mumbled words profound—

"ABRACADABRA"
BRACADABR
RACADAB
ACADA
CAD
A!"

That made the carpets leave the ground—

And twelve little girls were on their way—

To surprise their parents on Christmas Day.

Miss Clavel again quite well

Thought it time to ring her bell

Which quickly broke the magic spell.

And now we're back, all twelve right here

To wish our friends a HAPPY NEW YEAR!

Help Madeline fly home to her Christmas tree!

Color by number.

1. Gray   2. Yellow   3. Purple   4. Light Blue   5. Orange

These colors are only suggestions.
And it's okay to color outside the lines, too.

Circle the words hidden in the puzzle below.

Gift

Cup

Santa

Tree

A	T	P	M	O	U	S	E
W	R	I	A	F	E	H	L
Z	E	L	G	I	F	T	R
Y	E	L	I	E	O	D	I
B	V	O	C	X	R	U	G
K	W	J	I	U	L	N	A
U	Z	D	A	H	P	R	X
J	S	A	N	T	A	W	B

Mouse

Tiger

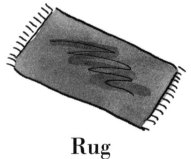
Rug

Girl

Magician

9

Recipe for Madeline's Cinnamon Bread

Ingredients:
4 slices of your favorite bread
butter or margarine
1/3 cup sugar
1 teaspoon cinnamon

Directions:
Ask an adult to pre-heat the oven to 350°.
Mix cinnamon and sugar together in a bowl.
Butter the slices of bread and put them on a baking sheet.
Carefully sprinkle the cinnamon and sugar on the bread.
Bake in oven 5–7 minutes or until the sugar is melted.

Can you find five mice hidden in the picture below?

Find the picture in each row that's different from the others.

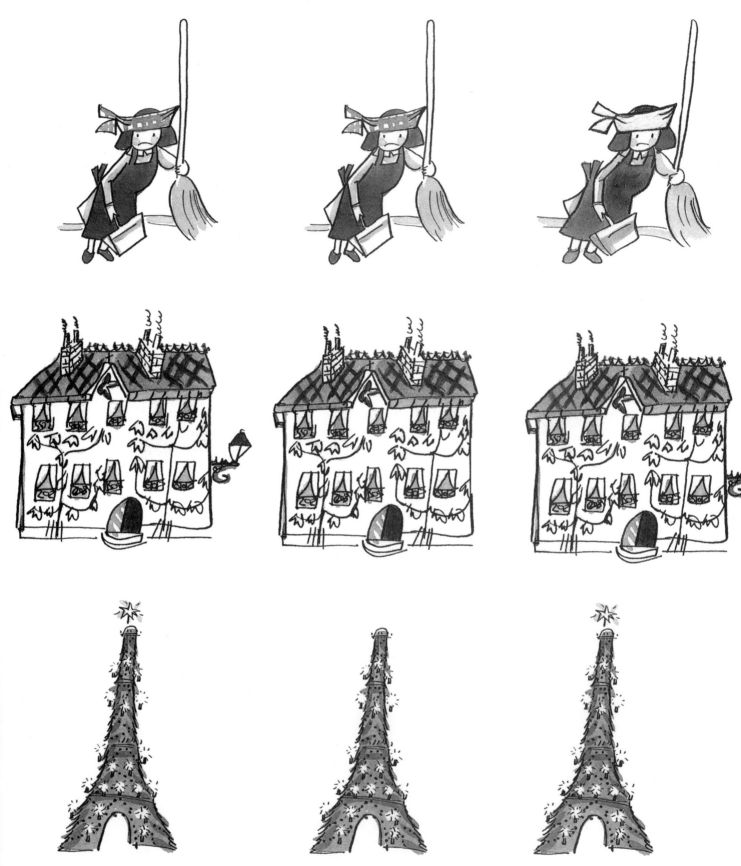

Match the item in the left column
with the place where it belongs in the right column.

Connect the dots.

Make an ornament to hang on your Christmas tree.

1. Color in the pictures.
2. Cut out along the solid lines.
3. Fold along the dotted lines to form a pyramid.
4. Tape the flap to hold the ornament together.
5. Ask an adult to make a loop through the top of the ornament with a needle and thread. Tie the loop and hang the ornament on your tree!

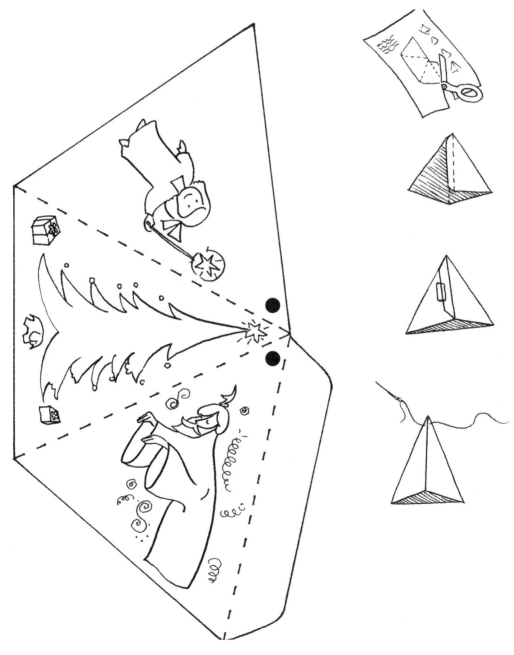

Answers

Madeline Christmas Activity Book copyright © Viking, a Member of Penguin Putnam
Books for Young Readers, 1998

Madeline's Christmas, *Madeline's Rescue*, and *Madeline and the Bad Hat* copyright ©
Ludwig Bemelmans, 1956, 1951, 1956
Copyright renewed
Art for *Madeline Christmas Activity Book* by Jody Wheeler

Special thanks to Ella, Thomas, and Jack Cahill, Tasha and Miika Greenwood,
Nina Robinson and Melissa Sweet
ISBN 0-670-88204-6

Viking
A Member of Penguin Putnam Books for Young Readers
345 Hudson Street
New York, New York 10014

Printed in U.S.A